MONTEZUMA
AND THE FALL
OF THE AZTECS

MONTEZUMA
AND THE FALL
OF THE AZTECS

ERIC A. KIMMEL

illustrated by DANIEL SAN SOUCI

HOLIDAY HOUSE / *New York*

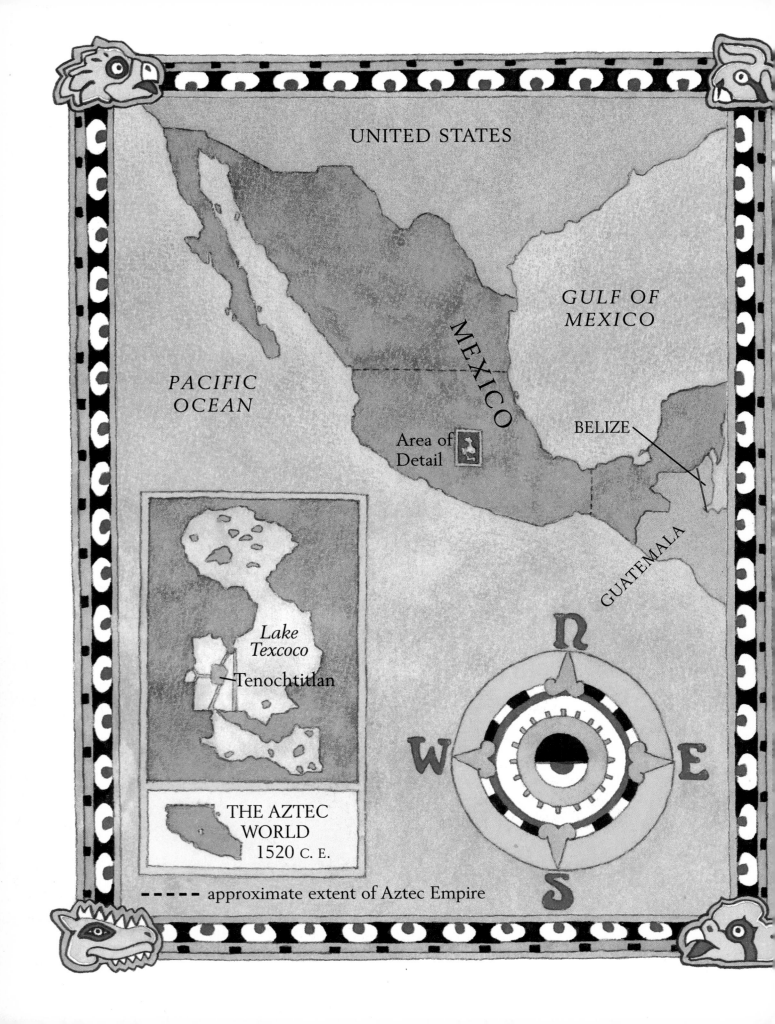

UNITED STATES

PACIFIC
OCEAN

MEXICO

GULF OF
MEXICO

Area of
Detail

BELIZE

GUATEMALA

*Lake
Texcoco*

Tenochtitlan

THE AZTEC
WORLD
1520 C. E.

- - - - - approximate extent of Aztec Empire

N
W   E
S

MOTECUHZOMA XOCOYOTZIN, known in American history as Montezuma II, became ruler of the Aztecs in 1502. The Aztec empire then covered most of what is now central and southern Mexico. Tenochtitlan, its capital, was one of the world's largest cities. It had more people than London or Paris.

But all was not well in Montezuma's domain. The Aztecs had built their empire by conquering other peoples. They forced the conquered people to give them gold, jade, incense, colorful feathers from tropical birds, and food. They made them send their handsomest youths and most beautiful maidens to Tenochtitlan to be sacrificed to the gods.

The Aztecs believed that the gods had to be fed every day. Otherwise, they would die and the world would end. Blood, the "precious water" of life, was the gods' food. The Aztecs sometimes went to war just to capture enemy warriors to offer to the gods.

Montezuma was a powerful ruler, but he was unhappy. He thought that the world was ending. The Aztecs believed that four other worlds had existed before this one. Each had been destroyed in a terrible catastrophe. Now there were signs that this world was about to end, too.

Strange voices were heard in the night. A temple caught fire and burned to the ground. The waters of the lake that surrounded Tenochtitlan suddenly rose and flooded the city. Stones spoke. Strange birds appeared. The Aztecs believed these mysterious events foretold approaching disaster.

One day a man came to Montezuma. He said that while walking near the ocean he had seen floating mountains. Montezuma sent messengers to investigate. They came back and told him, "We have indeed seen floating mountains, as well as men fishing from a small boat. These men are not like us. They have light skins and long beards. They are like no men we have ever seen."

Montezuma decided to treat these strangers as guests until he learned more about them. He sent his messengers back to the coast with rich gifts of gold, feathers, and jade. "Go swiftly," he said. "When you meet the strangers, tell them that Motecuhzoma Xocoyotzin sends them these gifts and welcomes them to his country."

The messengers returned, terribly frightened. "We met the strangers. They are more terrible than our war god, Huitzilopochtli. We presented our gifts to their leader, but he demanded more. When we told him we had no more to give, he put us in chains. He lit a metal tube that shot out a stone ball with a shower of sparks. It made such a roar that we fell down in terror. The strangers had huge dogs as fierce as jaguars. They rode on powerful animals like deer, but without antlers. Who could possess such wonders?"

The smoking tubes were cannon, the deerlike animals were horses, and
the floating mountains were sailing ships. As for the strangers, they were
Spanish adventurers led by a nobleman named Hernán Cortés. Cortés had
already fought a battle with the local peoples. Cannon, guns, and the sight
of men on horseback caused their warriors to flee in terror. Cortés believed
that with these "secret weapons" he could defeat any army that might
come against him.

A young woman named Malinche helped Cortés speak with the people of the coast. She explained that the conquered peoples longed to break free from Aztec rule. Cortés realized that the Aztec empire was not as powerful as it seemed. He decided to march to Tenochtitlan, capture Montezuma, and replace him.

Cortés burned his ships so there could be no retreat. Every man in his small army understood they had to win, or die. Cortés marched inland, accompanied by soldiers from the coast. More soldiers from other groups joined them along the way, eager to help fight the Aztecs.

Montezuma called a meeting of his nobles to decide what to do. Some wanted to attack the invaders at once. Others wanted to lure them into the city where they could be surrounded and captured. Montezuma decided to welcome them to his capital.

The Spaniards entered Tenochtitlan on November 8, 1519. Montezuma and his nobles came out to greet them. Montezuma hung a gold necklace around Cortés's neck and presented him with gifts of jade and jewels. He gave the Spaniards a palace and assigned servants to look after their needs.

Cortés, however, did not trust the Aztecs. Montezuma appeared to be friendly, but should he ever turn against them, the Spaniards would be trapped inside the city. Cortés decided to spring his own trap first. He marched to Montezuma's palace and placed the Aztec ruler under arrest. Surrounded by Spanish soldiers, Montezuma had to surrender.

Thousands of Aztecs filled the streets as word of Montezuma's capture spread through the city. Cortés realized he could not fight them all, so he ordered Montezuma to speak to the angry crowds. Montezuma told his people to go home, telling them he was not a prisoner, but had come to visit the Spaniards as their guest. The Aztecs obeyed Montezuma this time, but they were not deceived. They realized the terrible truth—their ruler had become a hostage.

With Montezuma in his power, Cortés began to do as he pleased. He took over the royal treasury, invaded the temples, and threw down the statues of the gods. He ordered human sacrifices to cease. Each act increased the hatred the Aztecs felt for the invaders. They waited for the moment to strike back.

Word arrived that another group of Spaniards had landed on the coast. Cortés feared that this new group might try to take the Aztec empire away from him. He left Tenochtitlan to deal with the intruders.

While he was gone, the soldiers he left behind attacked a religious procession, murdering six hundred Aztec nobles and priests. Tenochtitlan was about to explode.

Cortés defeated his Spanish rivals. He returned to Tenochtitlan to find his palace surrounded by furious Aztecs, eager for war.

What happened next is unclear. Spanish writers say that Cortés ordered Montezuma to command his people to return to their homes. But Montezuma could no longer control them. The Aztecs threw stones and shot arrows at their former ruler. Badly wounded, Montezuma died three days later on June 30, 1520.

Aztec writers tell a darker story. They say the Spaniards murdered Montezuma in a dungeon cell, then dumped his body in a canal. The truth will never be known.

With Montezuma dead and the entire Aztec nation fighting against them, the Spaniards could no longer stay in Tenochtitlan. Cortés and his men fought their way out of the city at night in a driving rainstorm, leaving their gold and their wounded behind. The survivors fled across the bridges, stumbling over the bodies of the dead.

Spanish writers call that terrible night *La Noche Triste*, the Night of Sorrow. However, it was a great victory for the Aztecs. Cortés lost half his men and all his guns, cannon, and horses. Most of the native warriors who had joined him also perished.

But Cortés did not give up. He returned to the coast to organize a new army and plan a second attack on Tenochtitlan.

This time, all the peoples conquered by the Aztecs sent armies to help Cortés. Tenochtitlan was completely surrounded. The Spaniards cut off the city's supply of food and fresh water. Hunger, thirst, and disease, especially the devastating smallpox, took the lives of thousands of Aztecs. Yet they refused to surrender. Led by a heroic young prince named Cuauhtemoc, Montezuma's nephew, they drove back the Spaniards again and again.

Four months after the siege began, the Spanish won. The great city of Tenochtitlan lay in ruins. Dead bodies filled the canals. It is believed that 240,000 people lost their lives.

The Aztec nation had come to an end. A new nation, Mexico, was about to be born.

Author's Note

In 1520, the native population of Mexico numbered 25 million. One hundred years later it was barely one million. An entire civilization perished forever.

Some blame Montezuma for the disaster. Had he attacked the Spaniards with all his force when they first entered his realm, he might have wiped them out and ended the threat to his nation. Others disagree. Cortés's little army was a tough fighting force. Though vastly outnumbered, it was never defeated in open battle. Even if the Aztecs had eliminated Cortés, another Spanish army would surely have come to take its place.

It is important to remember that Cortés did not really "conquer" the Aztecs. What he did was start a revolution and put himself at the head of it. The Totonacs, Tlaxcalans, and other subject peoples who joined Cortés against Montezuma did not realize they were replacing one tyranny with another that would prove to be far worse.

Cuauhtemoc, the heroic prince who continued to fight the Spanish after Montezuma's death, was the last hero of the Aztecs. He is honored today as the first hero of Mexico.

Glossary

Cuauhtemoc (Kwow-TAY-moc)—Montezuma's nephew, last ruler of the Aztec nation

Hernán Cortés (Er-NAN Cor-TEZ)—conqueror of Mexico

Huitzilopochtli (Weet-zeel-o-POCH-tlee)—the god of war; principal god of the Aztecs

Malinche (Ma-LEEN-chay)—former slave who became Cortés's interpreter and advisor, also known as Doña Marina (DOH-nya Ma-REE-na)

Motecuhzoma Xocoyotzin (Mo-tay-cu-ZO-ma Sho-coy-OH-tzeen)—ruler of Mexico at the time of the Spanish Conquest; commonly known as Montezuma (MON-tay-zu-ma) or Moctezuma (MOC-tay-zu-ma)

Tenochtitlan (TEH-noch-tit-LAHN)—capital of the Aztec empire. Mexico City, the capital of present-day Mexico, is built on the ruins of Tenochtitlan.

For Further Reading

Berdan, Frances F. *The Aztecs of Central Mexico: An Imperial Society.* San Diego: Harcourt Brace Jovanovich, 1982.

Carrasco, Davíd and Eduardo Matos Moctezuma, eds. *Moctezuma's Mexico: Visions of the Aztec World.* Niwot, Colo.: University Press of Colorado, 1992.

Davies, Nigel. *The Aztecs: A History.* Norman, Okla.: University of Oklahoma Press, 1986.

Diaz del Castillo, Bernal. *The Conquest of New Spain.* Trans. by Cohen, J. M. New York: Penguin, 1983.

Gruzinski, Serge. *The Aztecs: Rise and Fall of an Empire.* New York: Harry N. Abrams, 1992.

Hassig, Ross. *Mexico and the Spanish Conquest.* New York: Longman, 1994.

Leon-Portilla, Miguel, ed. *The Broken Spears: The Aztec Account of the Conquest of Mexico.* Translated by Lysnder Kemp. Boston: Beacon Press, 1992.

—. *Aztec Thought and Culture: A Study of the Ancient Nahuatl Mind.* Norman, Okla: University of Oklahoma Press, 1963.

Smith, Michael E. *The Aztecs.* Oxford: Blackwell Publishers, 1996.

Thomas, Hugh. *Conquest: Montezuma, Cortés, and the Fall of Old Mexico.* New York: Touchstone, 1993.

The author and illustrator would like to thank
Professor Michael E. Smith, Ph.D., of the Department of Anthropology,
University at Albany, State University of New York, for all his help.

To the people of Mexico—E. A. K.

For Jim Lamarche and Norm Green,
two of my favorite illustrators—D. S. S.

Library of Congress Cataloging-in-Publication Data
Kimmel, Eric A.
Montezuma and the fall of the Aztecs / by Eric A. Kimmel;
illustrated by Daniel San Souci.—1st ed.
p.   cm.
Includes bibliographical references.
Summary: Traces the life of the last emperor to rule the Aztec empire
in Central America before it was conquered by the Spaniards.
ISBN 0-8234-1452-3
1. Montezuma II, Emperor of Mexico, ca. 1480–1520 Juvenile literature.
2. Aztecs—Kings and rulers Biography Juvenile literature.
3. Aztecs—History Juvenile literature. 4. Mexico—History—Conquest, 1519–1540
Juvenile literature. [1. Montezuma II, Emperor of Mexico, ca. 1480–1520.
2. Kings, queens, rulers, etc. 3. Aztecs Biography. 4. Indians of Mexico Biography.
5. Mexico—History—Conquest, 1519–1540.]
I. San Souci, Daniel, ill. II. Title.
F1230.M6K56   2000
972'.018'092—dc21
[B]   99-37134
CIP